WE MAY NOT ALL BE HEROES

A COLLECTION OF RICKMONISH SHORT STORIES

SIERA LYNN

First published by Autumn Moon Studio 2023

This novel is entirely a work of fiction. The names, characters, and incidents portrayed in it are the work of the author's imagination. Any resemblance to actual persons, living or dead, events or localities is entirely coincidental.

First edition

Cover by Casey Gerber

Map Illustration by Rachael Ward

Cultural Consultation by Nala Wu

ISBN 979-8-89034-359-8 (PBK.)

ISBN 979-8-89034-360-4 (HC)

ISBN 978-1-08811-915-0 (EPUB)

For Aaron, Adam, Avis, Chris, Daniel, Edward, Joey, Lis, Madelyn, Sage, Steph, Therin, and all those that have helped to bring the world of Rickmonish to life in all its forms.

THE GREAT CITIES OF
RICKMONISH
MAJOR CITIES
MINOR SETTLEMENTS
THE CELMENISTY SEA
FLARINSIA
EBKANOR
BULMELDA
KYRO

SYNTHGRAB
MIGHTDENN
MENTANOS
NARMUR
MIROS
VENTANOS
WINDRANE
THE FLIMPATH SEA

CONTENTS

INTRODUCTION

In 2020, I embarked on a journey to bring a world to life through the tabletop roleplaying game Dungeons and Dragons. I have always been a profound lover of fantasy and storytelling, and as I began collaborating with my friends at a table, rolling dice, and going on adventures, the world continued to take shape.

Now, on its third iteration as a campaign, the country of Ebkanor on the continent of Rickmonish has come to life as a podcast and actual play stream. I've had 15 players help me get the world and its characters to the point they are today, and I would not be here without them.

Ebkanor is an experimental utopia where all persons are treated as equals, there is free education and a universal income, guards are mental health professionals, and there is free housing for all. But it has not always been this way. There was a time when there were one hundred years of war. The people of Ebknaor could not see their adversaries, but they tried to fight. One woman has been said to end the war, a great knight with terra-cotta skin and umber hair. She fell from the sky like a comet creating a great desert in the country's middle. She was found by a ranger exploring the desolation and nursed back to health. She called herself Mysheria and disappeared. The same day she disappeared, the invisible adversaries vanished, so the religion of Mysheria was born and swept through all of Rickmonish.

This collection of stories spans decades and cultures. Villages and Planes, and yet, for those who know the world, the names will be familiar.

Just as players have rich backstories for their characters, earnest growth, and cornerstone moments that make them who they are, so do the non-player characters; these are their stories.

I

YOUNG

A small, thin child runs through the woods while a man with an axe yells after her, "I'm going to get you!"

Weaver laughs, stumbling over a vine that catches her toe as she looks back toward the burly man. His linen pants and frock are blowing in the crisp fall wind.

Weaver ducks to the right and presses her back to a large maple with red and yellow leaves. She hugs her rag doll close. Rosalyn is her most precious possession, on this particular day at least. She tries her hardest to slow her breathing but can't as she runs further into the woods, laughing as she goes.

The man whispers now, his boots crunching the fallen leaves as he tries to quiet his steps.

"I smell a child!" he yells as he turns around the corner of the tree, raising both hands overhead, axe in one and the fingers of the other rounded into claws.

The girl screams, yelling back toward the man through giggles and heavy breathing, "You can't catch me!" She stands as quickly as possible, fumbling with Rosalyn.

Her long black hair hangs in braids around her oval face. She keeps throwing them back over her shoulder, so they are out of her way as she sprints back to the house.

Just steps from where the forest floor breaks onto a pathway leading to the cottage, the man wraps one strong, hairy arm around her. He rolls her up in his arm and tosses her over his shoulder.

"I caught you!" he yells as she kicks and giggles and screams into his torso.

"Daaaaaddddd. You're supposed to let me make it back to the cottage," the child cries, still resisting his hold but to no avail.

"Oh, no, no, no," the father explains. "Now I get to have fresh pies just like the fairy queen! Little girls make the best pies." He smacks his lips together as one does after a delicious meal.

Weaver yells, cries, giggles, and kicks as her father takes her inside, and they plop onto the large hand-made bed they share. The candle on the wooden table is about to burn out. Its flame, only a few inches from its metal holder, lights the space in the sunset.

They both laugh and smile, and slowly the tiny child removes herself from her father's embrace and grabs a flax cloth apron from the wall.

"What shall it be tonight, Father? Apple turnovers? Hazelnut cake? What about chocolate croissants? I still haven't made so many of Mama's recipes." She grabs a leather-bound book from a shelf on the wall and begins leafing through its pages with the most tender care.

The man looks at his daughter as she stands sil-houetted in the reds and oranges of dusk by the oven he made for her mother. At that moment, he remembers how much this child looks like her Mama, from the pinch of red on her nose to the olive wash of her skin.

"Well, Weaver, I always did love her chocolate croissants."

2

RUN

Blood splatters Mif's face from a new death to his right as he runs open-mouthed through a field. The wheat reaches up to his shoulders. An arrow pierces his flesh, lodging in the soft place between his chest plate and shoulder piece. He can no longer pull his arm down to his side. His hand bounces limply at the end of the dangling, useless appendage as he continues to run.

What point is there in fighting? he thinks between heartbeats as he runs. *We can't even see them.*

He cannot breathe.

He cannot feel his body.

He cannot blink or stop.

He can only run.

He trips. His usable hand meets something soft and wet. There is a squishing sound as he stands again, pushing off what feels like the studs of leather armor.

A tall man with gangly arms and bovine-like ears runs into view. As he strides toward Mif, arms waving and yelling, Mif watches as his torso is separated from his hips. Both fall forward, the torso hanging in the air for far too long in his vision.

Mif's ears are ringing.

He makes it to a road where a pony with no rider rears and snorts, unsure of what to do. He raises his hand.

"Shhh. Shhhhhh," Mif coos to calm the beast. He struggles to mount the animal with one arm but, with some effort, gets himself astride.

He grabs mane and rights himself on the creature.

"Ha," he yells, and off they run. He does not care where. He's not sure why he is even trying.

No one can see the enemy.

They cannot beat them.

Nowhere is safe.

He does not steer the pony in any direction and instead allows it to run where it would like. He barely stays conscious, but when he can focus on the world around him, he catches flashes of greenery, stars, and sunrise.

Finally, the pony halts, and as Mif opens his eyes, he looks into a spring with small, winged, sharp-teethed, glowing creatures swimming in its waters. He drops from the animal's back and falls onto the sandy shore, the water's edge centimeters from his head. He tries to hold onto the present moment and the world around him, but its colors slowly fade into the black void that obliterates his vision.

MIF WAKES UP, wrapped tightly in blankets and bandages, lying on a cot in a dark room—a small ray of light streams in from a hole in the ceiling.

"You are awake," the old woman says. There is a

shake to her voice, and she approaches him with a wooden bowl filled with dark green paste. She has gray hair and faded orange, pink, and blue wings.

The man recoils slightly and winces in pain. He looks down to where he remembers an arrow once protruding from his shoulder and sees nothing but bandages against where his arm used to be.

He begins to weep.

"You are alive," is all the woman says.

Mif sobs as the woman replaces his bandages, smearing the green paste on the place where his arm once connected to his torso. Her face is filled with kindness, focus, patience, and love as she tenderly administers her care. Mif watches her and notices a sort of orange shimmer around her being. Her kindness and care do not pull Mif from his despair.

"I don't want to be," the man whispers between hitched breaths after she has finished.

The woman moves to a door-like opening in the cave they are staying in. Mif watches the pixies swim in the water on the other side of the opening as he realizes they are held at bay with a magical barrier. The pixies are drawn to the woman, illuminating her as she moves her bowl of soiled bandages through the magical threshold, washing them in the water at the cave's opening. Not a single drop of liquid enters the cave.

"Do you have no one that loves you? No one you love?" she asks, her eyes shining in excitement and anticipation.

"Not anymore."

"That is not true," she purrs. The man looks in

her direction and watches as a soft shimmering of pink, blue, and orange magic swallows the space where the older woman stands. As it dissipates, he finds a young, beautiful woman standing where she had been.

This is still her, Mif realizes.

A shock, a jolt of electricity, streaks through Mif's head and heart. As he is enveloped in warmth and love, he smells a sweet stout, hears laughter and music, and feels giddy butterflies begin to stir in his loins. He does not resist the magic. He instantly loves this woman and knows that she loves him.

"What is your name?" she asks.

"Mif. Please, call me Mif," he replies with a small, shy smile. How good it feels for him to smile again.

3

TOGETHER

"I have something blue!" yells Zara from the hallway.

Aurora Ralona looks into the only mirror at the inn. She didn't sleep well, and dark bags formed under her eyes pronounced even in her warm black skin.

Today is her wedding day.

Aurora thought she would be filled with glee, pride, excitement, and butterflies. Instead, she finds herself full of deep and unrelenting sadness.

Zara enters the room with a kind smile and arms full of supplies. She puts down her materials and begins placing two aventurine earrings through the holes punched in her sister's ears.

"Aurora, you haven't said a word in an hour. Is everything okay?"

Zara places herself between her sister and the mirror.

Aurora looks down at her own hands, which have formed into a ball, her thumb rubbing the fatty part of her opposite hand in a comforting gesture.

"Rori, come on. What's wrong? Please, talk to me." Zara takes Aurora's hands.

Aurora bites her lower lip, breathing in deep sighs and sniffles. She finally looks at her sister.

"I miss them so much, and even more today," Aurora says quickly.

Zara's face softens as tears stream down her sister's face. No longer able to keep her mask in place, she feels her tear ducts opening.

Seeing her sister cry has always had power over her.

"Oh, Rori," Zara sputters and engulfs Aurora in a tight hug, mindful of the loosely tied coif of coily curls they had oiled to perfection earlier that morning.

Aurora sobs into her sister's shoulder.

"You know they would love to be here, and that they love you, and that they wouldn't want you to be sad for them on your wedding day," Zara comforts her twin, but to no avail. Her voice breaks as the last words fill the room around them.

They hold each other and walk to the bed, where they help each other sit down. They stay there for a while as each sister holds space for the other's mourning.

They have done this many times before. In the 160 years since their parents went to war and disappeared, there have been many milestones in their lives that their parents could not attend. It's as if neither person existed except in Zara and Aurora's memories.

No letters.

No reports.

No bodies.

No funeral.

Zara wipes her eyes, crosses the room, and grabs a small cloth from her nightstand. Returning to her sister on the bed, Zara dabs the tears from her face.

"Philip is a kind, intelligent, sweet, caring man who loves you with his whole being. Mother would have loved him. Father would have been hard on him but they would discuss magic in the evenings around the fire. Mother and Father would have snickered every time he tripped on a stone in the path and smiled whenever they saw him reach for your hand. They would have seen your love and been happy that you found it. They would be happy, Aurora. They would be proud. They would." She stops and looks at her sister.

"I know," Aurora says, and a small smile brings light to her face. "I know."

4

ALONE

The rain falls in sheets as Ghesh, a red-scaled, dragon-like teen, slips through the shadows in an alley as he follows a halfling woman. Her bag hangs off her shoulder, and Ghesh sees it is full of food. His mouth begins to water at the thought of a bite from a fresh apple. He imagines the crunch as his teeth break through the skin. The juice running down his chin.

Without hesitating, he jumps next to the woman from the shadows. She screams, dropping her bag and running from Ghesh out of the alley.

Ghesh grabs a bundle of strawberries from the bag and finds a place to sit behind a few crates. His soaked and dirty cloak hangs heavy on his body, squelching against the stone wall as he leans back.

He shovels the strawberries into his mouth. His stomach turns a bit as the food hits his belly. He hasn't had fresh fruit in a week or more. He eats greedily as his thoughts rush in.

That woman screamed. The guards will be coming. I have to keep moving or be put in the system. Mom always said, "Never let them put you in the sys-

tem. Never let them know you have nothing and no one to return to."

His mind reels as he thinks of his mother's dying wish. He wants to keep his promise to her, but he has grown weary of most of what she taught him about Ebkanor in the four years since her passing. Her experience in Bulmelda was with a different place with a different history and different government. He has made friends in Flarinsia that live in their own homes with gold in their pockets and food in their cellars because they signed their name on a paper at the city building, entering the system his mother so vehemently distrusted.

Ghesh remains here in the alley, gobbling up berries as if he has never tasted them, thinking of his life if he were to break his promise to his mother.

After a few minutes, finished with the strawberries, he looks through the bag again, finding cocoa beans in the bottom. He settles back behind the crate, and his stomach aches as he eats the chocolate, savoring every bite.

His vision plummets into darkness as he places one of the last pieces of chocolate into his mouth. He has only heard of this type of darkness, the darkness of magic—and as soon as he realizes that this magic most likely comes from a person, he runs.

He leaves the bag where it lies in the alley, soaked through from the rain, and sprints, following the path the woman had taken only minutes before. He looks back to see a single guard dressed in a rose-pink uniform. The guard yells back to a whole squadron behind him. He is the only one that pursues Ghesh.

"Stop! Wait!" the guard yells, pausing momentarily to drop the darkness spell.

Ghesh does not stop. Instead, he makes a hard right turn and scrambles up a ladder with extraordinary ease. The guard remarkably continues to follow close.

Ghesh reaches the top to find nothing but a door that leads down into the building. He paces the roof's perimeter, gauging a possible jump to an adjacent structure, but he cannot find one that looks safe. The door is his only hope for an escape without a fight.

He returns to the door and tries to pick the lock just as the guard hoists himself onto the roof.

The guard holds up his hands and moves hesitantly closer to Ghesh, his pink uniform sticking to his skin. He sputters rain away from his mouth as he speaks.

"Hey. Kid. Did you jump a halfling woman in the alley? All that was in her bag was food. Do you need food?"

"Just going to take me in, put me in the system like you do everyone else? Make me disappear?"

Ghesh doesn't look back as he speaks to the guard, barely believing the words coming out of his own mouth. Instead, he listens and twists his metal tools in the lock. He struggles to keep his grip on the smooth metal instruments drenched in the wet and chill of the rain.

"Are you not currently in the system? Is that why you are on the street?"

Ghesh looks back at the guard, this time with a bit of surprise. The kindness and confusion on the guard's face give Ghesh pause.

Maybe this is my chance? Maybe I can have a bed of my own...But I can't betray my promise.

"I'm on the street because bastards like you put

people into the system, and they disappear. I'm on the street because my parents left me with nothing, and I traveled here for a better life only to be told I have no skills and to join the system. I refuse to be a cog in someone else's machine," Ghesh speaks with growing intensity, repeatedly vomiting out the words he has rehearsed in his mind until he hears a hard crack.

One of his tools breaks in his hand, and he stares wide-eyed. These tools gave him homes to sleep within, food to take as he pleased, and a warm place to wash when needed. He only borrowed the spaces and the belongings and always tried to leave them as he found them.

What will he do now? He has no coin to purchase another set of tools.

The guard takes a few steps closer to Ghesh, seeing the shock and fear on the Dragonborn's face.

"Look, kid, Do you need a warm bed, a meal, some fresh clothes, a bath? How about I let you come back to the hall for the night? I can tell you what it means to be put in the system, and from there, you can decide what you'd like to do. Sound fair?"

It has been a very long time since Ghesh has seen that someone is simply offering him help.

I'm sorry, mother. I have to do what is best for me. Please, forgive me.

"Okay." Ghesh sputters away the rain. "Okay, but you have to stop calling me kid." His hands shake as he drops his broken tools to the ground and follows the guard back down the ladder.

"I am also going to have to get you signed up for some community service for robbing that woman, but we can talk about that in the morning."

5
WOW

The pork is warm and flavorful, floating in a gravy atop a mountain of potatoes. Kevin, his mother, father, and mastiff dig into a hearty, home-cooked meal.

"How was the shop today?" his mother asks between bites. She uses a knife and fork to place some potato and meat on top of a flaky biscuit.

"It was good. Maria came in for a new dress for herself and pants for Nathanial. She is always so sweet, but it took the rest of the linen I had in the shop to cover them. I will need to go to Flarinsia in the morning to refresh my stock of fabrics." Kevin's father's voice is kind but gruff. His mustache moves up and down in a funny way, seemingly tickling his upper lip as he chews his food and looks toward Kevin.

"And how was your day today, son?"

Kevin smiles at his father and pulls a few sizeable red maple leaves from his pants pocket. He throws them in the air and giggles as they slowly sway side-to-side, floating down to the floor and the table.

"Playing in the leaves again, I take it?"

Kevin smiles again at his father, and the mastiff approaches, hopping up so that his front legs rest on Kevin's lap. The dog begins licking the boy's brown-skinned face as he laughs. Kevin leans back to escape the licking attack and falls with a clatter. The whole family is laughing now as Kevin pushes the dog aside and pats him on his head.

"Fred, get down." Kevin's father shouts.

"Are you all right, dear?" Kevin's mother says through giggles as they all calm their laughter. Kevin rubs the back of his head but smiles again, nodding to assure her.

After dinner, they clear the table, and Kevin helps with the dishes, allowing the warm water to wash over his skin, the coarse fibers of the cloth engrossing him as he works. After every dish, he rubs the rag up his arms to experience the fibers on his skin.

Not long after that, the family settles into the living area where the fire Kevin's father has made is burning brightly in the hearth. In her favorite rocking chair, his mother begins to read Kevin a story from a children's book collection, and it's not long before Kevin is asleep on the rug, the dog curled up behind him.

Kevin's father gently carries him to bed, tucking him in before heading to his room.

A few hours later, Kevin wakes, his mouth very dry. He blinks his eyes a few times to get rid of the fog in the room, but when the scent of ash hits his nose, he realizes this is no fog. This is smoke.

He hears the scratching of paws on wood, and after grabbing a blanket off his bed, he stumbles to the door, feeling dizzy and light-headed. He opens it to find his dog lying on the hall rug crying and whimpering while flames glow brightly outside the fireplace in the downstairs living room. They fully consume where he had been sleeping not hours ago, and the smoke billows in large clouds up the stairs.

Kevin pats his dog on the head, loses his balance, and braces a hand against the wall. The dog whimpers again at his feet, and Kevin sits on the ground to try to clear his vertigo. A few seconds pass, and no relief comes, so Kevin pushes on. He crawls on all fours over to the door down the hallway. He coughs loudly and pounds on the door with all his might. Fred scratches the door with his paws next to Kevin's small hands.

Kevin's mind is swimming in smoke as he coughs again. He tries the doorknob but is unable to open it. His mother and his father sleep behind that door.

KEVIN LOOKS over the railing opposite the door to the lower level of the home, completely engulfed in flame. His mother's rocking chair moves back and forth hauntingly as it burns.

What can he do? He cannot leave them behind, but he's not sure he will stay conscious much longer.

He pats his dog friend on the head and telepathically says, "Go get help, Fred. We need help."

Fred whimpers but bolts down the stairs jumping through the threshold half consumed in flame, and disappears into the night.

Kevin pounds on the door. His hands feel like boulders, and his eyelids slowly close.

He wakes to the moon shining above him, soft grass on his arms and legs, and a slobbery tongue on his face. He looks over to see his mother lying beside him, the frame of their smoldering home in the distance. He watches as her chest rises and falls with each breath, and as he looks behind her to what is left of their home, he sees a white-maned unicorn pulling his father from the fire.

"Wow," Kevin speaks out loud. His dog sits staring at Kevin turning his head from side to side.

6

TRANSFORM

A tall, proud wizard with midnight skin and princely hair stares into the vials lining his small workshop in the guest room of his city apartment. His red robes and hands are marred with deep charcoals and burnt plants. The shuttered windows of his workshop allow him to forget the passage of time as he works.

He pulls out a small paper packet tied with string. He unties the parcel and notices his name, Philip, scrawled hastily in charcoal on the paper.

Philip grabs the tongue barehanded from inside the packet, and his fingers burn. A hiss squeezes out between his lips as he drops the tongue onto the floor, its forked edge flicking and twisting as if it could escape. He wraps his burnt fingers in a cloth before grabbing a pair of rusty tongs and using them to slip the tongue from the floor into a vial he has pulled from the shelf. The tongue hastily disintegrates as a loud popping noise rings throughout the room, and the potion changes from soft pink to neon green.

"Perfect," Philip says as he moves across the room to a small section of cages. Various creatures cower in the backs of the square wire boxes. Philip opens one of the doors, fishing around with his free hand for the subject at the back. He pulls a warty gray toad from the cage and heads to a small clean table in the center of the room.

He whispers, "Stay put," to the amphibian as floating darkness moves from Philip's lips to the toad's ears. It stops its struggle against the half-elvish man as Philip begins to pour the potion over the body of the magically held creature.

The toad cannot scream, held by Philip's spell as excruciating pain ripples through her body. Her bones begin to crack and re-form, a sound heard throughout the room. Her skin regenerates, and her eyes change. The caged creatures whimper and slink further back into their prisons.

A beautiful green viper now resides on the table where the toad once sat.

"Philip Vastina!"

A pink-gloved fist pounds on the apartment door as a guard yells Philip's name.

"Mr. Vastina, open up! We have cause to search this apartment for evidence of the wrongful practice and experimentation in the creation of transmutation magic. You have one minute to open this door before we do so on our own."

"Fuck," Philip says under his breath, leaving the viper where it sits. He waves his hand at the ceiling while pulling a strange white flower from the pocket of his robes. The flower disintegrates at the wave of his hand, and Philip creates arcs of lightning that begin firing down on the room used for his research. Vials explode, creatures take their last breaths, and plant matter is vaporized as the magic beats down on every inch of the room. Philip barely escapes through the doorway himself.

He runs for a bookcase along a wall in the hall, whispers a passcode in Draconic, and disappears down a hidden exit. He had created this tunnel just for this moment. He doesn't hear the guards break down his apartment door.

Sometime later, Philip sits in a comfortable chair before a blazing fire on a cold winter night. Aurora sits across from him, looking at a ledger.

"Darling?" he inquires.

"Hmm?" she says without looking up at him.

"How would you feel about me taking your name instead of you taking mine? Philip Ralona rings so much better than Philip Torzumin."

7

HEIR

The vast library of the Mycelium Kingdon sprawls in front of King as he sits in his favorite corner chair. The smell of aged paper and burnt coffee wafts its way to him. A worried look shifts his long white beard as he contemplates the large, old book he has placed in a holder on the table in front of him. His gloved hands gingerly turn through its pages as he scans the words and illustrations for what he needs.

A way around this, he thinks. *Some way to save my daughter's life.*

The constitution of The Mycelium Kingdom brings him no hope as he sifts through its writings for the fifth time in so many days.

A purple mushroom in lavish sparkling robes walks toward him from around a bookcase. He does not acknowledge her.

"I appreciate your desire to find a loophole, King, but I knew the risk of this mission when I took it," she states in a tender, resonate voice.

He faces her, meeting her eyes and letting out a long sigh. She moves to his side, looking down at where he sits at the table. She notices the deep pockets under his eyes, the tangles and crumbs in his mustache and beard, and how his gills catch the room's candlelight. She breaks his gaze to grab a cup of water an attendant has left for him on a nearby table.

King turns back to the books.

"I will not have my daughter sent into this blasted war. We are not warriors. We are spies, observers, and historical chroniclers. It's no place for you. Keeper or no, this is not our fight, Assassin."

He rakes his hands through his beard and over his smooth cap. He meets her eyes again as she walks to where he sits with a cup in her hand.

"Father, I will be fighting to preserve our stories, our way of life. It is only a matter of time before the Gods also turn on us. They know we are here, and you've seen the reports. They are looking—actively looking—for this library, this tree. Other Planes are already feeling the reverberations. Let me do this for our people." She pulls his gloved hands from the book and kneels beside her father's chair. "Please, Father. Please, let me do this. Let us do this."

He holds her gaze for a long time. The conversations with Assassin over the past few days have devolved into heated arguments. King strives to protect what he loves the most, and she is his only heir to the Kingdom. It isn't until this moment, with her tender tone, his hands in hers, that he realizes that she will take up this mission regardless of anything he may find in his books. She made this deal and is determined to uphold her end of the bargain.

"I have never been to war" he quickly admits as

he squeezes her hands," I do not know what you will see, what you will find, or how to help you."

"I know," she holds his gaze.

"I cannot help you," King chokes on a small sob as the words rumble through his throat and out of his mouth.

"I know," she repeats, squeezing her father's hand as he begins to cry.

8

TOURNAMENT

Carling sits on the knee of a halfling woman, her blond hair braided into pigtails that flow down to the small of her back. She begins bouncing on her mother's knee as she watches a red-haired halfling woman in black studded leather armor enter the arena for a dagger-throwing competition. A black leather baldric filled with sparkling steel daggers - a sapphire in each pommel - surrounds the woman's small but mighty body. Carling watches as she strides into the space, crowds cheering her name.

"Ella! Ella! Ella! Ella!" they cry in unison as the woman pulls out a dagger with a smile and raises it to the air. The crowd bursts into a ruckus of cheering and whistling as she does.

Carling tries to yell over the other voices, "Mom! Mamma! Mom!" She wiggles on her mother's lap until she stands on her knees, waving her arms in the air to try and get Ella's attention. Minutes go by as Carling yells and jumps on her mother's lap before her mom, Ella, looks directly at her and winks.

"Carling, let's sit down, okay," her mother, Ann,

asks as she picks Carling up, settling them into their seats to watch the competition.

Each round is more arduous than the last, as entrant after entrant throws their weapons toward the target. Ella, of course, makes it to the final round. The crowd is an eager and fickle beast that only Ella's wins and encouragement can tame.

Ella strides to her place next to her final competitor, a large half-giant man who wields sinister flame-shaped blades. He stands nearly seven feet tall next to Ella's small, three-foot form, but she is not intimidated or frightened. Her skill, she knows, can speak for itself.

A bead of sweat falls down Ella's temple as the spring sun beats down; it's an unusually warm day. Her arms ache from the efforts of the last hour.

They take their first throws. The man hits the target in the hand-painted red outer ring. Ella's dagger lands inches closer to the bullseye.

The man's second throw is farther out, and hits the bottom left corner of the target, barely in point counting range.

Ella bites her lip and exhales as her second dagger flies, the sapphire hilt gleaming in the spring sun.

Bullseye.

The crowd goes wild. Carling again stands on her mother's legs, wiggling in her arms and yelling in celebration with all the spectators around them.

The giant-like man stomps his way back to the throwing line. He throws his final dagger with a grunt and perfectly angles it in a way that knocks both of Ella's daggers out of the target. All three daggers fall to the dirt below the frame with a thud, and the crowd gasps.

He turns and shoots a cocky smile at Ella and the crowds surrounding him, raising his arms to the sky in a gesture of victory. The crowd stays unusually calm and still.

Ella says nothing and keeps her focus on the task at hand. She grips her final dagger in her left hand and feels the leather wrapping around the steel hilt. If Ella can hit a bullseye with this throw, she will be the five-time Whimsten Dagger-Throwing Competition champion.

The crowd is quiet around her, or maybe she can't hear them over her own heartbeat. Breaking through it all, Ella hears her daughter's voice calling from the crowd, "I believe in you, Mama! I believe in you!"

Ella smiles and lifts her dagger to aim.

Thank you, Carling.

The air is sucked from the arena as everyone holds their breath; the dagger's pommel shines blue as it spins toward the target. It hits just above the hilt of the man's vicious blade. From where Ella stands, it looks like another bullseye, but barely.

The crowd stays silent as an officiating member walks to the target and then back to where the two competitors stand.

He moves between the competitors and, using magic to amplify his voice, says, "The winner of the 140th annual Whimsten Dagger-Throwing Competition is...."

There is nervous shifting among the crowd as the officiate, a black-furred bear, lets his gaze travel through the crowd.

"Ella!"

9

TOMB

Thunder pulls his black-furred tail closer to his body just in time as a large round boulder races down the corridor past him and the rest of his team. His whiskers and ears twitch as a yell of pain echoes through the caves behind him.

He looks out from the nook he found in the wall to see his comrade, a round-faced elf with dark black shoulder-length hair and deep purple robes, laying on the ground of the tunnel stifling a scream. Another team member has run to her, their green skin flashing in the torchlight.

"Shit," the orc strains as they examine the elf's foot. They begin to pull bandages and salves out of their pack, and a deep golden-yellow magical fog slowly floats from the orc's hands into the elf's foot.

"We have to keep moving," Thunder says as he begins to walk in the direction the stone had come from.

"Thunder, we need a minute, please." A goblin man calls back from behind him, at the side of the other two party members.

"Fine," Thunder says without looking back at

them, "take your minutes, but I'm pressing on. We have no idea when those beasts will break down the door below, and I need these answers for my research."

"Thunder," the elvish woman yells, "don't be stupid. Just give me a minute." She tries to stand but winces in pain as she puts pressure on her once-smashed foot. The orc gives them all a look of worry.

"I can't do more here," they say in a pained but professional voice, "I need to save the rest of my resources in case something else happens."

"Fine." Thunder groans and looks back long enough to throw a glowing red vial from his pack at the elvish woman.

"Drink this and catch up. Quickly."

Thunder disappears up the corridor. His diamond-shaped pupils enlarge to cover most of the green iris as he snuffs out the torch he is holding. He creeps slowly past a few more traps—visible to him, even in the pitch black—and finds a sizeable glowing room of gold, art, jewels, artifacts, and history. Ornate art portraying the different phases of the moon surrounds the space, and the center is a large granite platform with a glass casket.

Thunder makes his way up the stairs to the platform; a shiver runs down his spine.

He sees a man's sunken, gray face through the glass. The teeth are exposed from centuries of decomposition, and the jaw hangs open. A crown of iron rests on the dead man's head, and a mantle of gold and cloudy silver gems is draped over his shoulders.

Thunder's feline-like ears twitch backward as he hears his team approach the room's entrance.

"Can you break this lock?" Thunder jiggles an

iron lock that looks to hold the glass top of the casket to the bottom.

"I'll do you one better," the goblin man says as he pulls a key from his pocket and walks to the casket. It is a perfect fit, and he carefully removes the lock. A spray of dust escapes from the casket as the lid is lifted.

Thunder begins a spell. Black liquid ink forms around his body and slowly seeps into the nostrils of the dead king. The orc gasps and runs toward the corner of the room, where they watch the matter floating out of the casket form into a wolflike dust creature that stands aggressively facing the party.

The dead king takes a deep breath in from deteriorated lungs.

"Where am I?" the king asks as he turns toward Thunder.

"Long story short, you're dead, and we need your help." Thunder gestures toward the dust creature facing the party, "Please, call off your guard dog, would you?"

10

FALL

"We will now hear from Arielle," a blue-winged woman calls out to the room from where she sits on a precipice.

Squib sits in the crowd staring hard at his sister as she slowly stands. Her strong black wings are shackled together by magic. He watches her wince as she moves, her copper hair falling in her face, her fawn skin streaked with purple and pink bruises.

Arielle surveys the room, her shoulders slump slightly as she lets out a deep breath and looks up to the council member that had asked for her to speak.

"I will not stand before this council and say that I am content with my actions in the Battle of the Lavender Bridge. I cannot say I did not act selfishly when I was left alone with the commander in the hospital tent. I can share my story with sheer honesty and reflection. I hope the testimonies of others over the last few days will not cloud your ability to listen openly and without judgment."

Squib watches his sister, his jaw clenched and throbbing from stress.

Arielle continues, "It was the Third Sline of the

battle when I heard a commotion outside the hospital tent. I went to see what was the matter, and I saw my brother, Squib, lying face down in the purple mud with much larger men pinning his wings down as he struggled to breathe.

"I called out and moved closer to the soldiers. As I did, they began to jeer and slander me. Common threats that I have received because of my last name. I entered hand-to-hand combat with one of the men who refused to release the wing of my brother, not in response to their insult but in defense of my sibling.

"As I took the lead in the fight, I could see he would not relent. As a doctor, I had been holding back. It was never my intention to badly wound or kill this man. I wanted them to leave my brother in peace.

"Seeing the burning rage inside the soldier's eyes, I knew I would need to do something more aggressive than I was comfortable with to stop the fight. I was about to punch his temple when a searing pain shot through my back.

"I looked down to see the steel of an arrow puncturing my chest under my left clavicle and turned to see Commander Edwards loosing the arrow."

"I was hospitalized for two days. I was tended to by other physicians who advised me repeatedly to forget and to move on because Commander Edwards was influential in the military and political arenas, but I struggled to let it go. Squib visited me both days, filled with remorse and shame over what happened.

"On the third day, I was cleared for work. The final battle began on the nearby bridge as I returned to treating minor scrapes and mishaps. I did all I could to help everyone brought to us. After hours of surgeries, amputations, stitches, magical healing, and death, Commander Edward was brought into the tent.

"All the while, I simmered on the advice given to me by my colleagues not to make a fuss about the attempted murder. The official report sat on my desk in my quarters, filled and ready to send off, but I was afraid. They had made me afraid. Afraid that even though this man had attempted to take my life over a skirmish with one of his privates, he would do so much more to ruin me. That he had the power to."

Some council members shift in their chairs as they continue to listen. Arielle continues to share her story with passion and fury.

"I am supposed to help people. I became a doctor for our army because I wanted to help bring peace. Bring about the greater good. But sitting on a cot in front of me was the antithesis of everything I thought we stood for, bleeding out and needing my care. I ushered him into a private room at his behest and threats. We moved folks who should not have been moved to make space for him. We even placed wounded soldiers outside the tent's warmth and shelter to accommodate his request.

"Only then was I able to evaluate his wounds. A clean rapier thrust through the chest. It had chipped his rib and collapsed his lung. A deep slash across his gut caused his intestines to hang in the night air. My expertise is gut wounds, and as I told him we would need to sedate him for surgery and that our magics could not heal such grave wounds fast enough to keep him alive, he spit in my face. He yelled and screamed in pain and told one of my nurses that they were to get another doctor.

"I knew he had mere minutes before he would

meet death. I froze. The hatred grappled with me. I battled my desire to let him die and my need to serve and save. I froze too long. I motioned for the nurse to get another doctor, one he would approve of, and by the time they made it to the room, it was too late."

Arielle looks at her hands.

"That is how it happened."

The blue-winged council member stands, "You may kneel once more."

The council deliberates for hours in front of the spectators, in front of Arielle, in front of Squib, the family of Commander Edwards. Mrs. Edwards smiles smugly with a new fiancé sitting beside her. They all sit in silence and listen until the blue-winged woman speaks again.

"Arielle Malefis, you are dishonorably discharged from service for your negligence as a medical doctor at the Battle of the Lavender Bridge. For your assault of a lesser officer, you will pay a 1,500 gold fine. For the death of Commander Edwards, we find you guilty of the highest charge—Murder. You will be exiled to the earthly plane, and your wings will be taken."

There is a gasp throughout the room as a gavel hits wood. Two guards take Arielle's arms and begin to lead her to where her wings will be removed from her body. She hangs her head in resignation. Mrs. Edwards sneers at her as they drag Arielle across the room.

Squib stands, pushing through the crowd and running toward Arielle, "I volunteer to take her charges in her stead! Take my wings instead!" he yells.

The crowds grow silent once more, moving to allow Squib to be seen by the council.

"This is all because of me," Squib yells. "Let me volunteer in her stead."

The blue-winged woman nods, waving for the guards to stop hauling Arielle across the room. The council deliberates quickly.

"Very well. We will grant Arielle the grace of companionship. You shall be exiled together to the Material Plane, and Arielle may keep her wings while you forfeit yours."

"Thank you. Thank you, your Grace." Squib exhales and is brought into the room to take his sister's place.

About the Author

Siera Lynn is a storyteller, writer, and author of the new collection of short stories, *We May Not All Be Heroes*. She began writing while in college and started the Dungeons and Dragons game that inspired the world of Rickmonish in 2020. A full-time producer for TTRPGs, Lynn and her partner call the Seattle area home. You can visit her online on Twitter (@mystic_musings_)

www.ingramcontent.com/pod-product-compliance
Lightning Source LLC
Chambersburg PA
CBHW061145160726
48006CB00038B/2277